To SUZENE-
STAY
STICKY!.

[signature]

Sticky
Graphic
Novels

TIMBER

Dale Lazarov & Player

TIMBER

Script and art direction by Dale Lazarov
Additional script ideas and art by Player
©2016 Dale Lazarov & Player. All rights reserved.

StickyGraphicNovels.com

Printed and distributed by
ComicMix, LLC.,
304 Main Avenue, Suite #194,
Norwalk, CT 06851.
http://www.comicmix.com

Printed in USA.

Hardcover ISBN: 978-1-939888-51-8

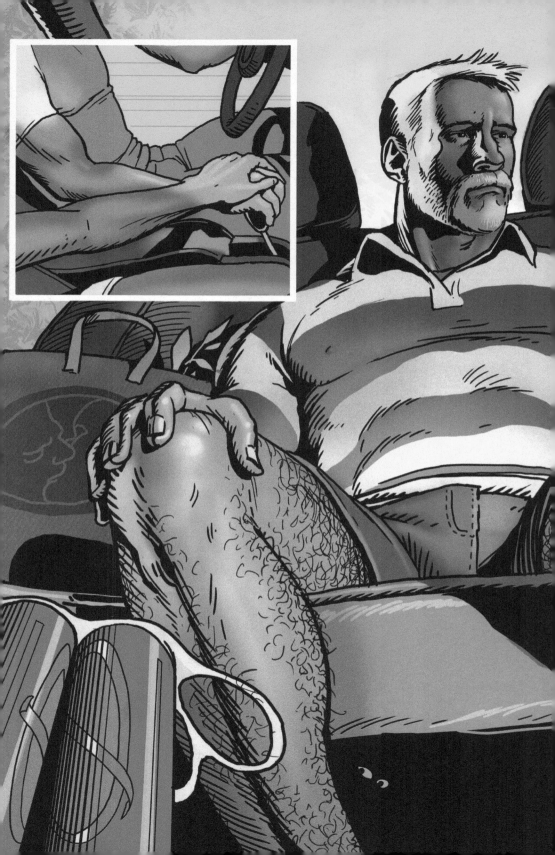

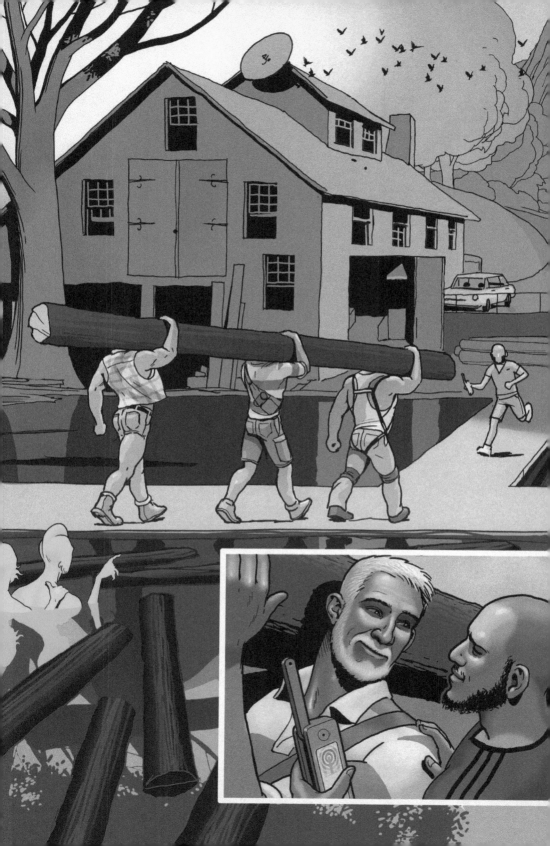

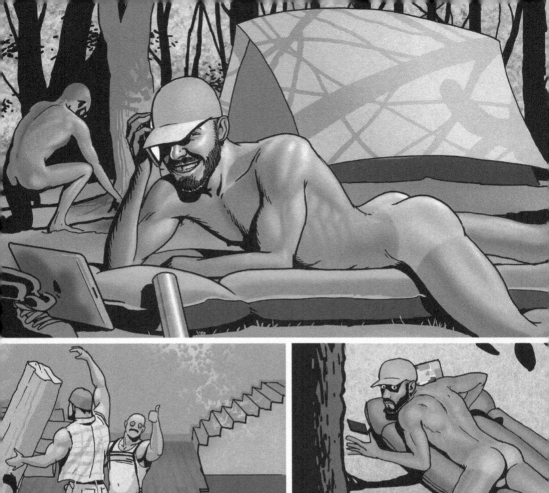

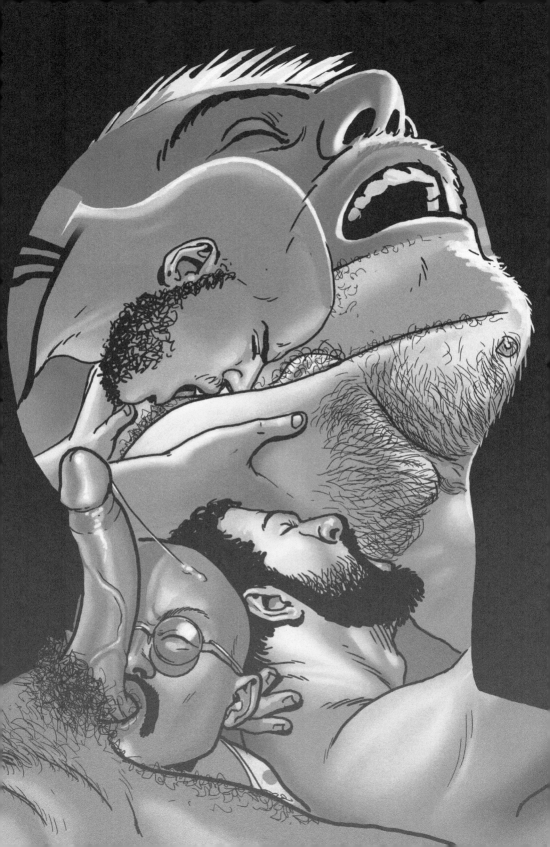

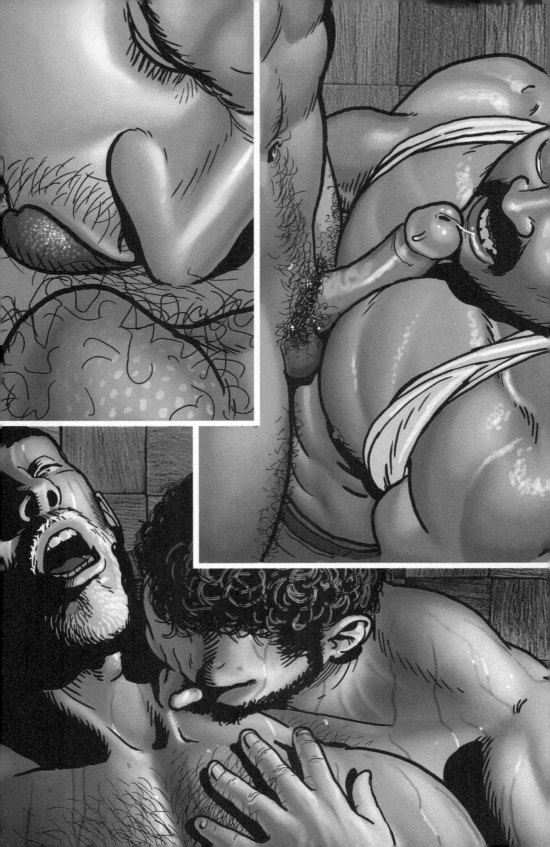

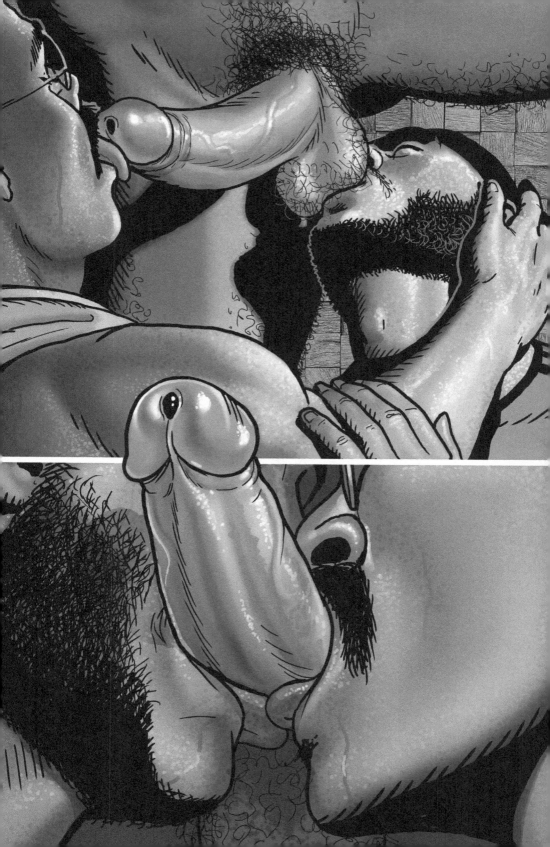

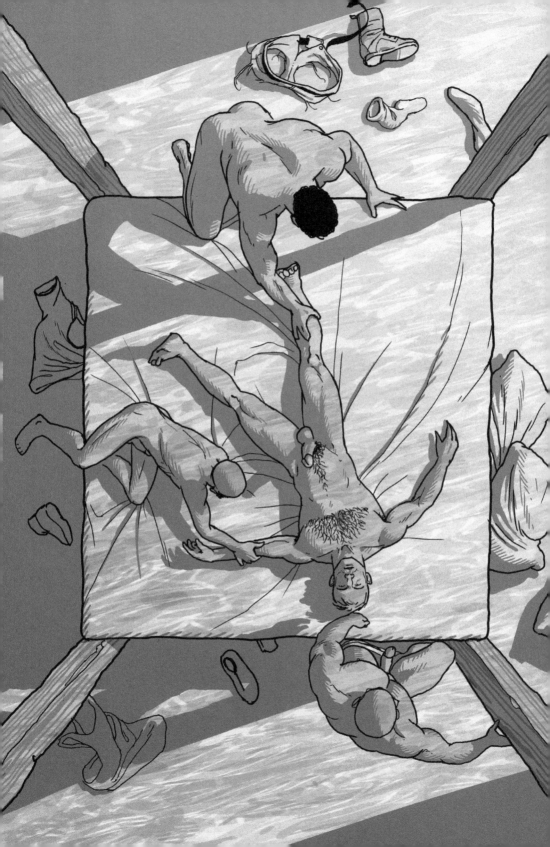

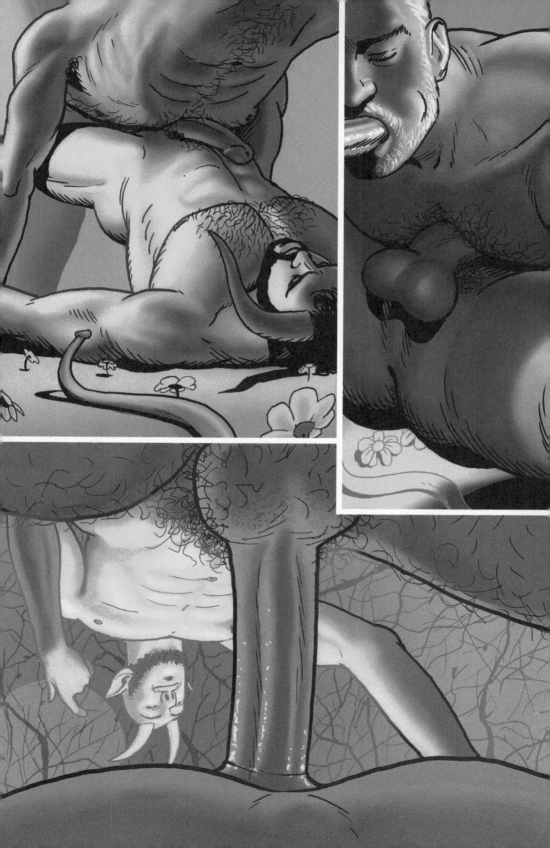

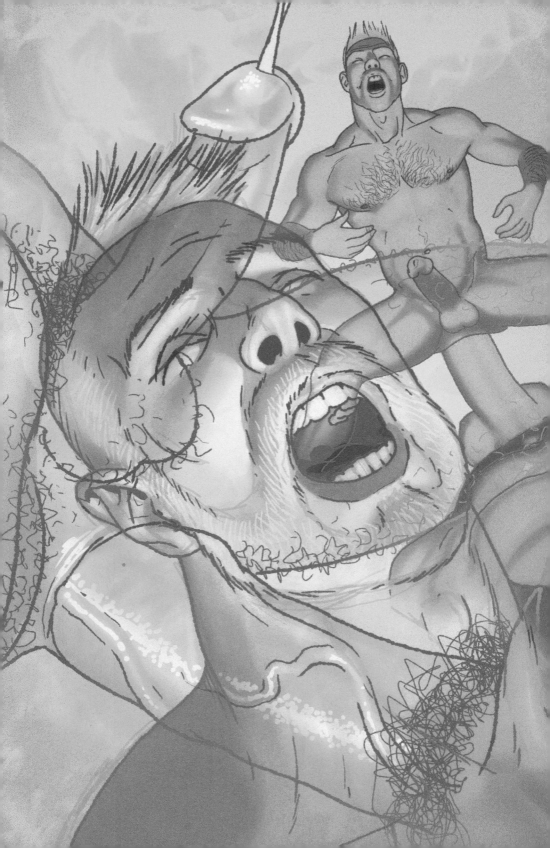

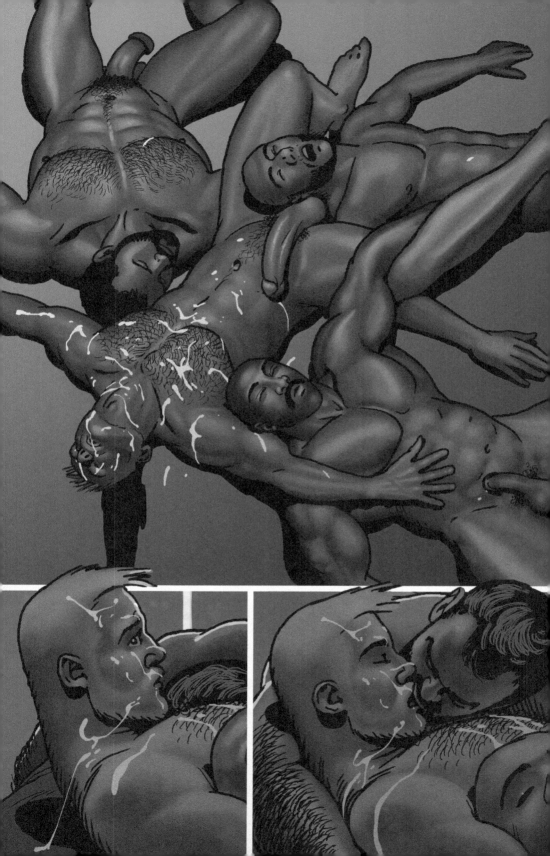

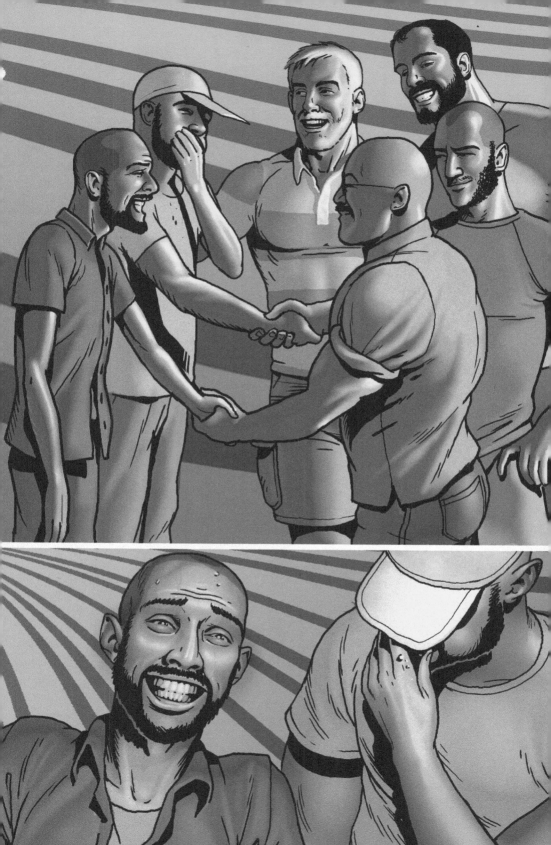

TIMBER
script/art direction: Dale Lazarov
additional script ideas/art: Player

About The Authors:

Dale Lazarov is the writer/art director of CARNAL (drawn by theAmir), SLY (drawn by mpMann), BULLDOGS (drawn by Chas Hunter & Si Arden), PARDNERS (drawn by Bo Revel), PEACOCK PUNKS (drawn by Mauro Mariotti), FAST FRIENDS (drawn by Michael Broderick), GREEK LOVE (drawn by Adam Graphite), GOOD SPORTS (drawn by Alessio Slonimsky), NIGHTLIFE (drawn by Bastian Jonsson), MANLY (drawn by Amy Colburn), and STICKY (drawn by Steve MacIsaac) — wordless, gay character-based, sex-positive graphic novels published in hardcover by ComicMix and in digital format through Class Comics. He lives in Chicago.

Player is a British illustrator who now lives, paints and teaches in San Francisco with his partner Dave.

CPSIA information can be obtained
at www.ICGtesting.com
Printed in the USA
LVHW07*1704060918
588589LV00004BA/16/P

9 781939 888518